THIS
$\mathcal{Treasury}$
BELONGS TO:

....

....

A Treasury Of ANIMAL TALES

This is a Dempsey Parr Book
Dempsey Parr is an imprint of Parragon

Parragon
Queen Street House
4 Queen Street
Bath BA1 1JE

Produced by
The Templar Company plc
Pippbrook Mill, London Road, Dorking
Surrey RH4 1JE

Printed and bound in Singapore
ISBN: 1-84084-485-X

A Treasury Of ANIMAL TALES

DP
DEMPSEY
PARR

Contents

★ The Three Little Pigs ★

Once upon a time there were three little pigs. They lived at home with their mother but as the years passed they grew bigger and bigger and soon it was time for them to find homes of their own. Their mother kissed them and waved goodbye.
"Watch out for the big, bad wolf!" she cried. Soon they met a man carrying a bundle of straw.

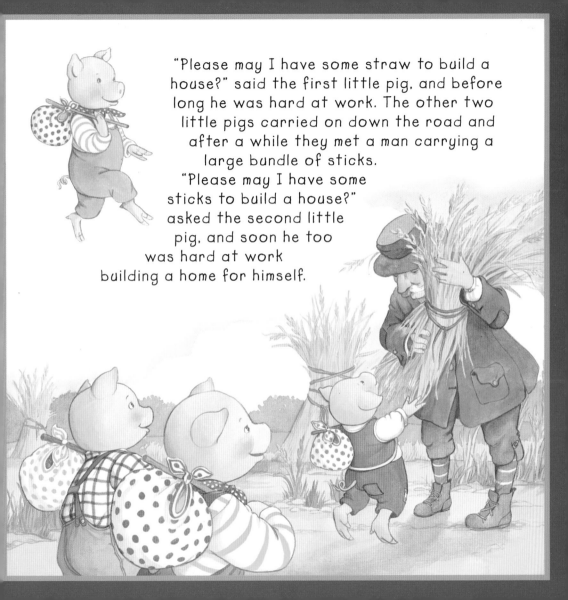

"Please may I have some straw to build a house?" said the first little pig, and before long he was hard at work. The other two little pigs carried on down the road and after a while they met a man carrying a large bundle of sticks.

"Please may I have some sticks to build a house?" asked the second little pig, and soon he too was hard at work building a home for himself.

The third
little pig carried
on down the road and
after a while he met a man
carrying a load of bricks.
"Please may I have some
bricks to build a house?"
asked the third little pig.
Soon he was very busy
mixing cement and laying
down brick
after brick.

The first little pig finished his house of straw and shut the door. The second little pig finished his house of sticks and shut the door. The third little pig finished his house of bricks and shut the door. "My house is good and strong," said each little pig to himself. "The wolf won't catch me now!"

But the very next day who should come calling but the big, bad wolf! Down the road he prowled, peering under hedgerows and pouncing behind bushes. He was very hungry and he wanted something to eat.

When he saw the little straw house, he was most surprised. "I wonder who lives here?" he said to himself and he peeked inside. How happy he was to see the first little pig digging into a large bowl of porridge.

"Little pig, little pig!"
he called.
"Let me come in!"
The first little pig
dropped his spoon
in fright.
"No, no! By the hair
of my chinny, chin,
chin I will not let you
in!" he shouted.
"Then I'll huff and I'll
puff and I'll blow
your house down!"
roared the wolf. And
he huffed and he
puffed and he blew
the house down and
in a flash he had
eaten the first little
pig all up.
Then he set off
down the road.

Soon he saw the house of sticks and how delighted he was when he spotted the second little pig sipping at a nice cup of tea.

"Little pig, little pig, let me come in!" he cried.

"No, no! By the hair of my chinny, chin, chin I will not let you in!" shouted the second little pig.

"Then I'll huff and I'll puff and I'll blow your house down!" shouted the wolf and sure enough, he huffed and he puffed, and he blew down the house in no time at all. Soon he had eaten the second little pig all up.

But when he visited the home of the third little pig he had a much harder job on his hands, for this house was made of bricks and however hard he huffed and puffed he could not blow it down. The crafty wolf sat on the gate and tried to think of another plan to catch the clever little pig. After a while the wolf knocked on his door.

"Oh, little pig," he called softly. "I know you like turnips and if you can be ready tomorrow morning at six o'clock then I will take you to Farmer Smith's field and help you pull some up." Well, the little pig was not going to fall for a trick like that and so he got up the next day and went to the field at five o'clock and was home cooking his turnips by the time the wolf knocked upon his door.

"You're too late," he called out. "I'm already cooking my turnips." Then the wolf gnashed his teeth and tried hard to think of another plan.

"Oh, little pig," he called. "I know you like apples, so meet me at Merrygarden Farm at five o'clock in the morning and I will help you pick some." The next day the little pig went to the farm at four o'clock but the wolf, too, arrived early and caught him up a tree!

"Here, catch!" cried the clever pig, and he threw an apple across the meadow. The silly wolf went bounding after it, and the pig went running home.

The wolf hid his anger and tried again. "Meet me at the fair at three o'clock" he said. But the pig went at two o'clock and bought a lovely butter churn. He was on his way home again when he saw the wolf coming up the hill towards him.

There was nowhere to hide and so he jumped inside his barrel and rolled down the road. He thundered past the wolf and the noise frightened the poor wolf so much that he turned tail and fled.

That evening the wolf knocked on the pig's door.

"A horrible monster attacked me today," said the wolf in a shaky voice, and then the pig laughed and laughed.

"That was me in my butter churn!" he said. The wolf was furious and he climbed up on top of the roof.

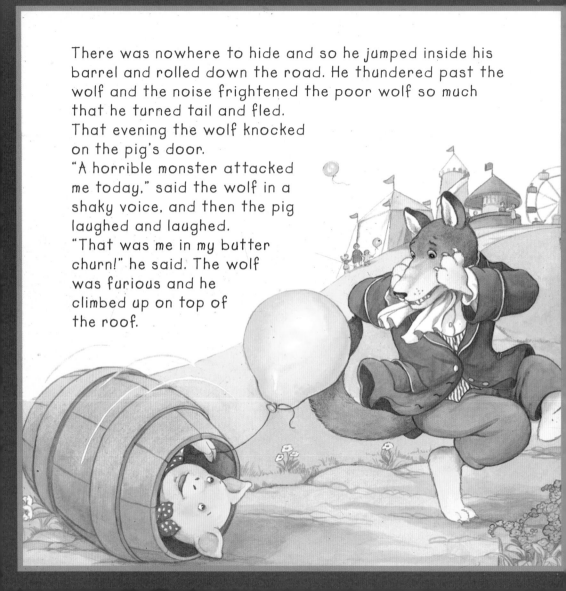

"I am coming down your chimney to get you!" he cried. Quickly the pig put a large pot of water on his fire and as the wolf scrabbled down the chimney it boiled up good and hot. Splash! The wolf fell in the scalding water and was dead at once, but the pig lived happily ever after.

★ The Hare and the Tortoise ★

There once lived a most bold and boastful Hare. He loved to stroll around the warren with his nose held high in the air, and it was evident to one and all that this Hare considered himself to be the finest Hare in all the land.

Now there was one thing that the Hare was proud of above all else. He had been blessed with strong back legs and that meant he could run like the wind. He never missed an opportunity to show off his running skills and no one had ever been known to beat him.

He had the pick of the crop in the cabbage patch because he always got there before anyone else. Early in the morning, while the other Hares were still sleeping he would scamper up the hill to the vegetable patch, eat his fill, then scamper down again. All that could be seen of the speedy Hare was a flash of white as his fluffy cottontail bobbed by.

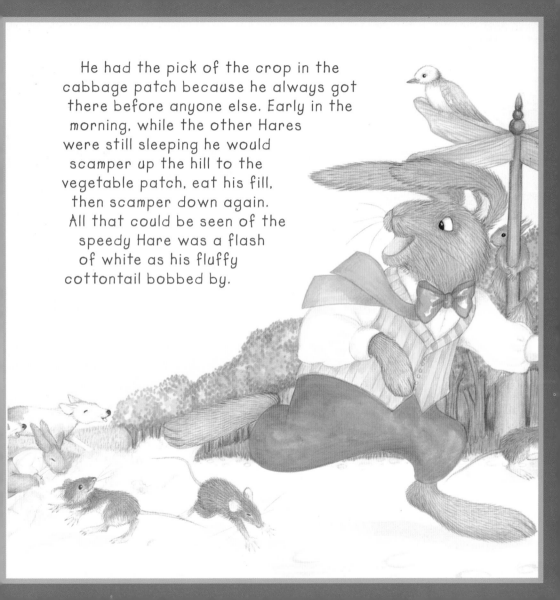

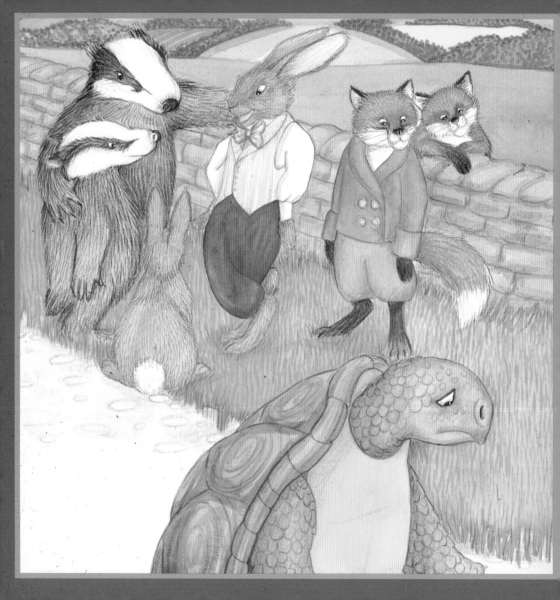

He was certainly a fine Hare and, with his long ears constantly twitching, he never missed a trick — at least, not until the day he met the Tortoise, who slowly crawled by as the Hare was bragging to his friends.

"Hurry up, hurry up, old Tortoise!" laughed the Hare. "If you went much slower the grass would grow over you!"

The Tortoise stared at him coolly.

"You may rush about all you wish," he said, "but I get to where I want to be soon enough, thank you." He looked the Hare up and down slowly before continuing. "In fact, I reckon I could get there quicker than you, fast as you are." The Hare burst out laughing.

"Quicker than me? That I should like to see! Nobody is quicker than me!"

"All the same," replied the Tortoise calmly, "I challenge you to a race. Name the time and the place and I'll be there."

The Hare thought it was very amusing that the Tortoise should want to race him, but he agreed all the same. The arrangements were soon made and the very next day everyone turned out to watch the Hare and the Tortoise run their race.
"Five, four, three, two, one, go!" cried the Fox, who was acting as umpire, and in a flash the Hare was out of sight and over the hill.

The crowd clapped and cheered as the old Tortoise lifted first one foot and then the other and slowly began to make his way along the path.

He looked neither right nor left but kept his eyes on the winding road ahead. But how could he hope to beat a natural athlete like the Hare? The Hare raced along and as he flashed by a great cheer went up from the people lining the road. It was obvious that the Hare was in a great hurry, but he still found time to turn and wave to his supporters as he ran by. Far behind him the Tortoise plodded steadily on his way.

Soon the Hare had reached the race's halfway point and he skidded to a stop.
"I have plenty of time," he said to himself. "I must be miles ahead of that old slowpoke by now. In fact, I could have a snooze right here and now and when I wake up, I would still have time to beat that Tortoise!"

So saying, he sat himself down under an old oak tree, leaned back and closed his eyes. Before long he was fast asleep and snoring!

The hours passed by and after a time the Tortoise appeared over the top of the hill. He ambled down the road until he reached the spot where the Hare was fast asleep. The Tortoise raised his eyebrows, but said not a word and without missing a step, continued steadily on his way.

On plodded the Tortoise, looking neither to the left nor the right, but just straight ahead, keeping his one goal in mind as the sun began to sink in the sky.

The air grew cooler and the Hare suddenly awoke with a shiver. He yawned, stretched and looked back down the road, and saw to his satisfaction that the Tortoise was nowhere in sight. "Still plenty of time to win the race!" said the Hare to himself happily. Up he jumped and off down the road he sped once again, but as he came over the top of the hill he saw the most amazing sight. There ahead of him was the Tortoise taking his last few steps towards the finish line! The crowds cheered wildly as his shiny shell broke the tape in two and the Fox declared him the winner. As the Hare panted for breath at the end of the race, the Tortoise smiled placidly. "Slow I may be but I keep my eye on the goal and I don't let anything distract me!"

And the moral of this story is:
"Slow and steady wins the race."

The Frog Prince

Once upon a time there lived a King and Queen. They had three beautiful daughters but the youngest Princess was so lovely that she warmed the heart of everyone who met her. She was a happy girl and her favorite toy was a golden ball which sparkled in the sunshine.

One hot summer's day the little Princess decided to play in the shade of the wood. She walked amongst the trees, tossing her ball in the air, until she came upon a glade where a fountain tumbled into a silvery pool. What a lovely sight! With a cry of delight, the Princess threw her ball high into the air and ran to catch it – but the ball slipped through her fingers, rolled over the ground and fell into the pool! With a cry of alarm she knelt by the pool and tried to reach it, but the ball sank from sight.

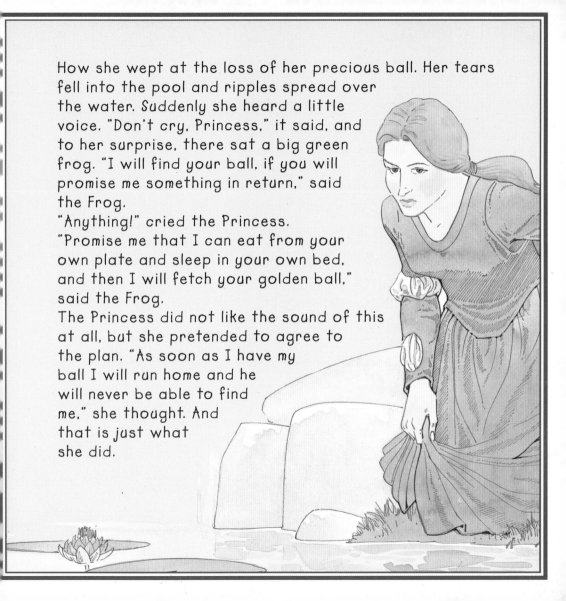

How she wept at the loss of her precious ball. Her tears fell into the pool and ripples spread over the water. Suddenly she heard a little voice. "Don't cry, Princess," it said, and to her surprise, there sat a big green frog. "I will find your ball, if you will promise me something in return," said the Frog.

"Anything!" cried the Princess.

"Promise me that I can eat from your own plate and sleep in your own bed, and then I will fetch your golden ball," said the Frog.

The Princess did not like the sound of this at all, but she pretended to agree to the plan. "As soon as I have my ball I will run home and he will never be able to find me," she thought. And that is just what she did.

That evening as the Princess sat down to eat she had forgotten all about the Frog. But the Frog had not forgotten her. He had found his way to the palace and at that moment was sitting outside the door. Suddenly the Princess heard a small voice.

"Open the door, my Princess dear.
Open the door to your true love here!
And remember the words that you and I said
By the fountain cool in the greenwood shade."

"Who is that, my daughter?" asked her father, the King. The unhappy Princess explained what had happened in the wood and her father looked grave.

"You must honor your promise," he said. "The Frog kept his word and now you must keep yours."

The Princess opened the door with a heavy heart and the Frog followed her in, flip, flop, flip, flop. The Queen, her sisters, and all the Ladies-in-Waiting shuddered with horror as the slimy little creature passed by, and when he hopped on the table they hid their faces in their napkins. The Princess wrinkled her nose in disgust as the Frog crept up to her plate and with a long darting tongue ate up her peas one by one. At last he sat back and yawned.

"Now I am sleepy," he said. "Please take me to your room for I wish to sleep upon your pillow."

The Princess was horrified. She looked imploringly at her father but the King shook his head. "It may seem hard, little daughter," he said, "but you must do as he asks. A promise is a promise."

So she carried the Frog upstairs and soon he fell fast asleep upon her silken pillow. The Princess vowed she would not sleep a wink all night but after a while her eyelids drooped and soon she, too, slept.

The next morning when she awoke the Frog was nowhere to be seen. "At last I am rid of the horrid creature," thought the Princess to herself - but she spoke too soon! That evening as she sat down to eat the same little voice called from outside the door.

There sat the Frog once again, and once again he asked to eat from her plate and once again the Princess had to do as he wished.

When he had eaten his fill he asked to be taken to the Princess's bed and there he slept as before upon her silken pillow. The little Princess had no choice but to lay by his side and she cried herself to sleep beside him.

The next morning when the Princess awoke, she opened
her eyes slowly, dreading the sight of the Frog beside
her. But he was nowhere in sight. Instead she found herself
gazing at the most handsome Prince she had ever seen.
"Sweet Princess," he said. "You have saved me from a
wicked spell. An evil witch turned me into a Frog and
banished me forever to the fountain pool. The only person
who could break the spell was a Princess who
would let me eat from her plate
and sleep on her pillow. You
have broken the spell and now I
am free." He knelt upon one
knee. "Please marry me."
The Princess agreed at once,
and after their wedding they left
in a beautiful white coach to
begin their new life together.

How the Camel Got His Hump

Now this tale tells how the Camel got his big hump.
In the beginning of years, when the world was so
new-and-all, and the Animals were just beginning to
work for Man, there was a Camel, and he lived in the
middle of a Howling Desert because he did not
want to work.
He ate thorns and tamarisks and milkweed and prickles
and was most 'scruciating idle, and when anybody spoke
to him he said, "Humph!" Just "Humph!" and no more.
Presently the Horse came to him with a saddle on his
back and a bit in his mouth, and said, "O Camel, come out
and trot like the rest of us."
"Humph!" said the Camel, and the Horse told the Man.

Presently the Dog came to him, with a stick in his mouth, and said, "Camel, O Camel, come and fetch and carry like the rest of us."
"Humph!" said the Camel, and the Dog told the Man. Presently the Ox came to him, and said, "Camel, O Camel, come and plough like the rest of us."
"Humph!" said the Camel, and the Ox went away and told the Man.

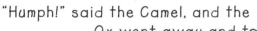

At the end of the day the Man called the Horse, the Dog and the Ox together, and said, "O Three, I'm very sorry for you, but that Humph-thing in the Desert can't work, or he would have been here by now, so I am going to leave him alone, and you must work double-time and double-hard to make up for it."

That made the Three very angry, and they held a meeting on the edge of the Desert. The Camel came chewing milkweed, and laughed at them, and said, "Humph!"

Now one day the Genie in charge of All Deserts came rolling along in a cloud of dust (Genies always travel that way because it is Magic), and the Three asked for help. "Genie of All Deserts," said the Horse, "is it right for any one to be idle, with the world so new-and-all? There is a thing in the middle of your Howling Desert with a long neck and long legs and he won't do a stroke of work."

"Whew!" said the Genie, whistling, "that's my Camel. What does he say about it?"

"He says 'Humph!'," said the Dog. "Nothing else, just 'Humph!'"

"Very good," said the Genie, clapping his hands. "I'll humph him if you will kindly wait a minute."

Then the Genie rolled across the desert until he found the Camel most 'scruciatingly idle, looking at his own reflection in a pool of water.

"You have given the Horse, the Dog and the Ox extra work, all on account of your 'scruciating idleness," said the Genie sternly to the Camel. "Humph!" the Camel replied. "I shouldn't say that again if I was you," said the Genie, and he began to work a Magic. Then the Camel said "Humph!" again, but no sooner had he said it than he saw his back puff up into a great big lolloping humph.

"That is your very own humph that you have brought upon your very own self by not working," said the Genie. "In future you will be able to work and work and work for three whole days at a stretch without having to stop and eat, because now you can live off your humph. Come out of the Desert and go to the Three, and behave." Then the Camel humphed himself, humph and all, and went away to join the Three. And from that day to this the Camel always wears a humph (but we call it a "hump" now, so as not to hurt his feelings).

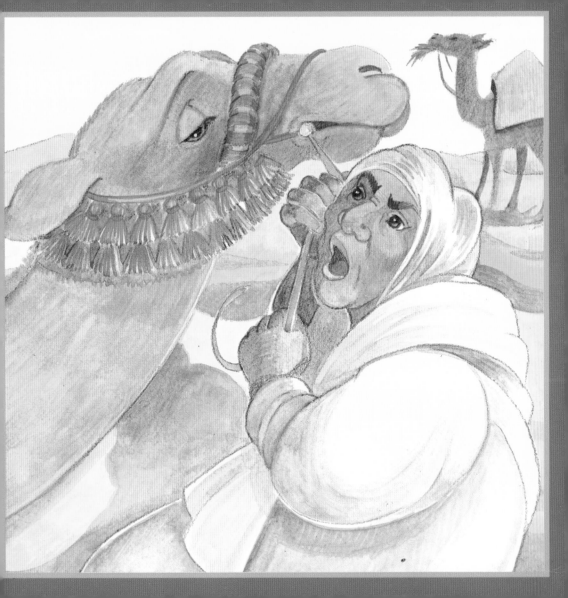

The Fox Without a Tail

There was once a fine Fox, a most handsome fellow, with a shiny red coat, beady black eyes and a long bushy tail. This Fox was a rather vain creature. Every morning he would gaze at his reflection in a large mirror and admire his good looks, and every night he spent long hours brushing his tail from top to tip until it shone like bright copper.

He spent his evenings prowling about and hunting along the hedgerows. Under the trees he slunk like a shadow and the leaves shivered as he passed by.

One cool evening, as the silver moon hung low above the horizon, the hungry Fox was out hunting for rabbits. Around the warren he crept on silent paws and deep in their holes the frightened creatures shook with fear.

But the greedy Fox was so busy thinking about what a tasty supper he would have, that he forgot something very important indeed...

He could be hunted too!
Suddenly a loud snap! broke
the silence and the Fox felt
the most terrible pain.
Twisting round he saw that
his fine full tail had been
caught in an iron trap!

The sharp teeth squeezed tightly on the thick red fur and the poor Fox howled in pain. He twisted this way and that in a desperate attempt to free himself but pull as he might, his beautiful tail was stuck fast.

Then all of a sudden the pain stopped. What a relief! But as the Fox looked behind him his jaw dropped open in dismay. The trap had pulled his tail clean off and the Fox saw it lying in all its glory upon the ground. This was a calamity! Why, he was a Fox! The best and finest Fox that ever was – and what was a Fox without his tail? Why, little more than a laughing stock! How the other Foxes would taunt him when they saw him creeping by, tail-less. The very thought of it was more than he could bear.

The poor Fox lay down, rested his head upon his paws and thought hard. He would have to think of a plan. He thought and thought, and by the time the moon was high in the sky he had decided what he should do.

After a while he stood up, collected his hat and made his way to the forest dell. Every night at midnight the Foxes would meet there to discuss any worries or complaints they may have.

There they all sat in a circle as the moon shadows spread over the ground. With his head held high, the Fox strutted into the center of the circle as a hushed silence fell on the entire company. He was wearing his best hat and tucked inside the hatband was his own fine red tail! Proudly he strutted before them and at last sat down on a bare rock.

Very quietly a young Fox began to titter, then another, then another and soon the forest rang to the hoots of laughter and rude catcalls which came from every side.

But the Fox simply lifted his nose even higher in the air and waited for the noise to die down. Then the Fox held up his hand for silence and spoke.

"If you are quite finished, I have something important to say," he began. "As you know, I have been blessed with a particularly fine specimen of a tail and I have been proud to carry it around behind me ever since I was born. But now I feel the time has come for a change. Tails should not drag behind us in the dirt where they could collect mud and dust. No, they should be worn on high, where their beauty can be fully admired."

There was a shocked silence as the Fox gracefully bent his head forward to show off his fine plumage, as he paraded around the glade. "From now on I suggest that all Foxes should remove their tails and wear them in their hats," he continued.
The other Foxes looked at one another in amazement.

"This is the new fashion," the Fox went on, "so you had all better start wearing your tails on your hats, like me, unless you wish to appear hopelessly out of date." Then the other Foxes began muttering amongst themselves, trying to make sense of what the Fox was suggesting. Surely he had taken leave of his senses to propose such a thing!

Then an old Fox rose creakily to his feet. "We have heard what you have to say, Brother Fox, but answer me this," he said politely. "Would you be quite so keen for us to follow this new fashion if your own tail had not been pulled off in a trap?"

Then the poor Fox realized that everyone had seen through his cunning plan and he slunk off into the forest, much ashamed. As the days passed he learned to live without his tail and no one thought any the worse of him.

And the moral of this story is:

"If you suffer some misfortune, make the best of what you have and do not try to make others suffer also."

The Ugly Duckling

There was once a little mother duck. She had six eggs in her nest and there she sat day after day in the summer sun patiently waiting for them to hatch. Five of the eggs were small and white, but the sixth egg was large and brown. The little duck often wondered why that egg was so different.

One morning she heard a crack, then another, then another. Her chicks were hatching! One by one they tumbled from their shells and soon five little chicks were gathered under the wings of their proud mother. But the large brown egg had not hatched.

"What can be keeping my last little chick?" thought the mother duck to herself and she settled herself on top of the egg to keep it warm.

At last she felt the egg moving and out scrambled a chick. But this chick was nothing like her other babies. He was covered in dull brown fluff and had a long scrawny neck. He wasn't nearly as pretty as his brothers and sisters. But the mother duck loved him just the same and took care to protect him from the other farmyard animals who often teased him.

"Did you ever see anything quite as ugly as that gawky looking creature?" squawked a large brown duck to his friend, the white hen.

"Go away!" clucked the hen. "We don't want you in our farmyard," and she pecked at the poor little duckling with her sharp beak.

Not a day passed by without one animal or another making fun of the duckling, so at last he decided he would run away. One dark night he crept away quietly while everyone was asleep and headed for the open fields. By daybreak he was quite exhausted.

"I will rest for a while," he said to himself and was soon fast asleep. But he awoke just two minutes later to feel the hot breath of a large animal wafting over him. Peeking out from under his wing he was terrified to see a fierce beast with a long red tongue! It was a hunting dog but to the duckling's great relief it simply sniffed him and then padded away across the moor.

"I am too ugly even for that dog to eat!" thought the duckling to himself sadly and he waddled off in search of somewhere to live.

Not far away there was a cottage and for a time the duckling stayed there with an old lady, her hen and her cat. But as the days passed he longed to find some water so that he could splash about and swim. "I must find a pond," he told the cat as he waved them goodbye. The weather grew colder and the snow began to fall. Suddenly the duckling heard a strange sound high above him and looking into the sky he saw a flock of white swans flying south for the winter. The duckling watched them go, spellbound. He had never seen anything so beautiful in all his life. "If only I could go with them!" he sighed, "but what would those lovely creatures want with an ugly companion like me."

On he trudged and at last he reached a little pond — but how wretched he was when he saw that the water had turned to ice! There was one small patch of freezing water and there he splashed for a while but the cold had sapped his strength. Soon he found he could not get out of the water and back onto the land. After a while the ice crept closer and closer and then he was trapped. The duckling would surely have died if a man had not happened to pass by at that very moment. He saw the little creature stuck fast in the ice and took him home and warmed him by the fire. So the duckling spent the next few weeks being cared for by the kind man and his wife.

Soon the weather grew warmer and the duckling longed to be on his way once again. "I must find a proper home for myself." he explained to the man and his wife as he waddled away.

The air grew softer, the birds sang and the flowers bloomed in the meadows once again. The duckling felt stronger and he noticed that his feet and his body had grown much bigger and seemed to be changing color. He felt happy and excited and, stretching out his wings, he beat them up and down for fun. Just imagine his astonishment when he suddenly found himself leaving the ground and flying through the air! What a glorious feeling it was to be soaring on high. "Here in the sky I am free!" he said to himself happily.

All at once he saw something exciting far below him. As he swooped down to get a better look he recognized the snow white birds who had flown over him on their way south. Now they had returned and were splashing in the pond. The duckling landed on the water and slowly swam towards them.

"I know I am ugly," he said shyly, "but please let me stay with you and be your friend."

"Why, you are not ugly!" laughed the birds. "You have become a beautiful swan just like us." and as the duckling bowed his head to look in the water he saw that it was indeed true!

THE WOLF AND THE ASS

The Ass was feeling very cross. The other animals had been teasing the Donkey, and as the Donkey was a close cousin of the Ass, they had been making fun of him, too.

Now it has to be said that the Donkey was not the cleverest of animals. He would happily spend hours passing the time of day with his reflection in the pond and he had long conversations with his shadow, who trotted alongside him.

But the Ass was quite a different matter. He was crafty and cunning and could not be easily tricked like his trusting cousin. He was very offended that the other animals should make fun of him. "One day they will discover that I am nobody's fool," he said to himself.

A few days later the Ass set off to find some sweet grass to eat. He followed the path from the jungle and soon found himself far away from his usual haunts. Here the grass was lush and green and soon the Ass was busy chewing away, quite contented and without a care in the world. The sun shone from a cloudless sky and the only sounds to be heard were the steady chomping of his teeth and the slow swish of his tail as it lazily flicked from side to side.

But as the Ass munched happily, he thought he heard a rustling sound. The Ass pricked up his ears and listened, but everything was silent and still.

Slowly he lowered his head and carried on grazing. But a few seconds later the Ass froze again, for this time he could hear the pad of soft paws behind him. The hair on his back prickled all the way from his long ears right down to his tail.

Nervously he looked over his shoulder.

There in the bushes he saw the gleam of the big gray Wolf's shining eyes.

"That Wolf means to make me his supper!" said the Ass to himself. "I must stay calm and think of something fast!" Soon he had thought of a clever plan to save himself. The Ass moved off in search of more sweet grass, but now he limped as he went along, and the Wolf crept like a shadow behind him. The Ass began to chew a fresh clump of grass, all the time watching the Wolf from the corner of his eye. The Wolf prowled nearer and nearer and his tongue hung so low he almost tripped over it. When the Wolf was close enough to pounce, the Ass lifted his head and called out quite calmly.

"I wouldn't do that if I were you," he said. The Wolf was astonished. Why was the Ass so unafraid?

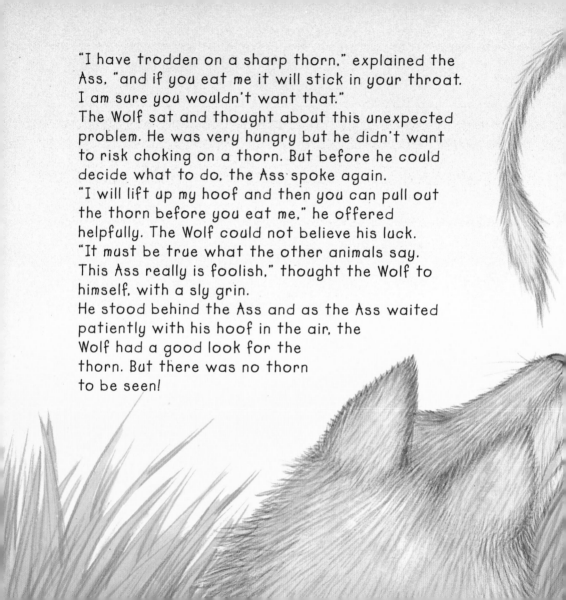

"I have trodden on a sharp thorn," explained the
Ass, "and if you eat me it will stick in your throat.
I am sure you wouldn't want that."
The Wolf sat and thought about this unexpected
problem. He was very hungry but he didn't want
to risk choking on a thorn. But before he could
decide what to do, the Ass spoke again.
"I will lift up my hoof and then you can pull out
the thorn before you eat me," he offered
helpfully. The Wolf could not believe his luck.
"It must be true what the other animals say.
This Ass really is foolish," thought the Wolf to
himself, with a sly grin.
He stood behind the Ass and as the Ass waited
patiently with his hoof in the air, the
Wolf had a good look for the
thorn. But there was no thorn
to be seen!

"Are you sure there's a thorn in your hoof?" called the Wolf.

"Quite sure," replied the Ass. "Take a closer look."

The Wolf bent down closer and peered at the hoof once more. Then the Ass summoned up all his strength and with a loud whinny he gave a mighty kick.

The Wolf flew head over heels into the air and landed in the middle of a thorn bush, howling with pain.

"That Ass is not as stupid as he looks," thought the Wolf to himself as he picked the thorns from his bottom, one by one, but the Ass just smiled at him sweetly. "I am nobody's fool," he said, and he trotted off home.

And the moral of this story is: "Beware of unexpected favors."

FISHING FOR THE MOON

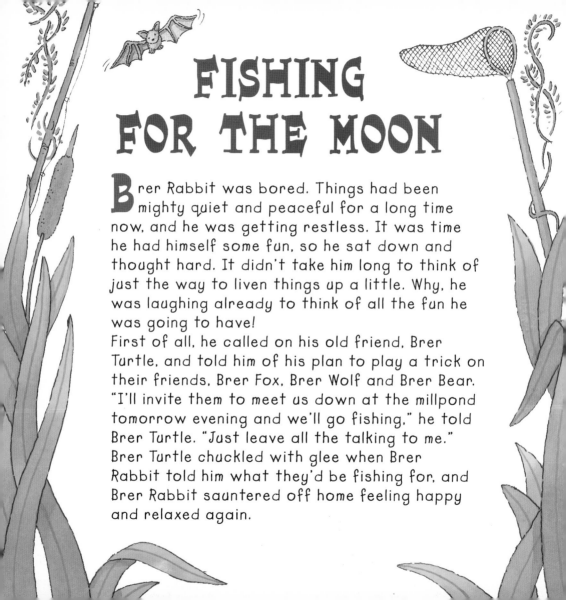

Brer Rabbit was bored. Things had been mighty quiet and peaceful for a long time now, and he was getting restless. It was time he had himself some fun, so he sat down and thought hard. It didn't take him long to think of just the way to liven things up a little. Why, he was laughing already to think of all the fun he was going to have!

First of all, he called on his old friend, Brer Turtle, and told him of his plan to play a trick on their friends, Brer Fox, Brer Wolf and Brer Bear. "I'll invite them to meet us down at the millpond tomorrow evening and we'll go fishing," he told Brer Turtle. "Just leave all the talking to me." Brer Turtle chuckled with glee when Brer Rabbit told him what they'd be fishing for, and Brer Rabbit sauntered off home feeling happy and relaxed again.

The next day Brer Rabbit called on the other animals and invited them to join the fishing party. They thought it was a fine idea, and so it was that they all met up on the edge of the millpond later that night.

Brer Bear brought a large net, Brer Fox carried fishing rods and Brer Turtle held a large box of wriggling maggots to use as bait.

"I'm gonna fish for mud-cats," said Brer Bear.

"I'm gonna fish for horneyheads," decided Brer Wolf.

"And I'm gonna catch me some suckers," Brer Rabbit whispered to Brer Turtle, with a wink. With that Brer Rabbit got ready to start fishing. But as he looked out over the water suddenly he jumped back with a start, and his eyes nearly popped out of his head.

He rubbed his eyes, and scratched his head in bewilderment as he stared at the pond.

"I reckon there'll be no fishing for us tonight," he said. "We might all just as well turn around and go home." Brer Turtle scrambled to the edge of the pond and peered over. He shook his head. "Well I never!" he said, most astonished. "What is it?" cried Brer Fox in alarm, as the others stretched their necks and peered into the darkness to see what the problem was. "I'm afraid the moon has fallen in the water," said Brer Rabbit, in a very serious tone. Everyone rushed to the waters edge and looked, and sure enough, there lay the moon quivering in the pond and the animals all tut-tutted and scratched their heads.

"Only way we'll get some fishing done tonight is if we get that moon out of the pond," said Brer Rabbit at last. "Isn't that right, Brer Turtle?"

"Oh, yes!" said Brer Turtle, nodding his head.

So the animals decided there was nothing for it but to take the moon out of the pond.

"But how shall we do it?" asked Brer Bear. Then Brer Rabbit closed his eyes and pretended to think hard.

"I have heard of this kind of thing happening before," said Brer Rabbit. "We'll have to use the fishing net to drag the moon out, and with any luck we may pull a big pot of money out with it. At least, that's what I've heard..."

Well, at that, Brer Fox, Brer Bear and Brer Wolf grew mighty excited.

"Why didn't you say so sooner?" said Brer Bear, and he stepped into the pond with a splash, closely followed by Brer Fox and Brer Wolf.

They dragged the net through the water and pulled it up. No moon! They tried again. Still no moon!
"You've nearly got it!" cried Brer Rabbit as he tried hard not to laugh.
Further and further they went until soon they were right out in the middle of the pond and here the water was deep and cold. Suddenly they were out of their depth and one by one their heads disappeared and bobbed up again as they thrashed the water with their arms. They splashed about so much it was a wonder they didn't empty the pond! Brer Rabbit and Brer Turtle laughed until they cried!

At last they scrambled
onto the bank, cold
and miserable.
"Better luck next time!"
said Brer Rabbit grinning
broadly and he winked at
Brer Turtle. Why, it was almost
too easy to trick those
silly animals!

Peter and the Wolf

There was once a young boy called Peter. He lived with his grandfather in a little cottage on the edge of a big dark wood in a country far away. They were a long way from the nearest town and there were no other houses nearby. Peter had no friends of his own age to play with and so he made friends with the animals that lived close by. His three best friends were a bird, a duck and a cat. The bird had a nest just outside his bedroom window and in the morning she woke Peter with her merry chirping.

"Come out and play, Peter," she would say. "The sun is shining and it's a lovely day." Then Peter would run outside and find the bird in the garden. Sometimes she would sit in the tall trees beyond and then Peter would open the gate and follow her into the meadow. But if his grandfather saw him he would be very cross.

"It is not safe in the meadow," he said. "Bad animals could come out of the wood and find you there. You should stay in the garden away from danger."

Outside the garden was a duckpond where the white duck lived. She would quack gently while Peter sat and fished, and they enjoyed each other's company.

Peter's third friend was his cat and she preferred to stay indoors in the warm kitchen. There she would sleep for hours on end, purring happily.

But Peter's three friends were not friends with one another! In fact, they did not like each other at all. They would not make friends with anyone but Peter.

Bright and early one morning Peter was woken by the little bird singing. "All is quiet, all is still," she called from the top of the tall tree in the meadow. Peter jumped out of bed, pulled on his clothes, and ran outside. He paused by the garden gate and looked out across the meadow. He remembered his grandfather's warning and shivered. Then he shook his head as if to clear it of any doubts. "What harm could come to a brave boy like me," he thought to himself and with that he pushed open the gate and slipped into the meadow.

He strode along whistling a merry tune as the bird flew about his head. There on the pond swam the little white duck. "Quack, quack!" she said happily when she saw him.

But the little bird was not pleased to see the duck. Angrily she flew over the white duck's head and chirped loudly in her ear. "Call yourself a bird? You can't even fly!" The duck shook her tail in fury. "Well, you can't swim!" she squawked crossly.

The bird twittered to herself as she flew back and
forth above the pond. And below her swam the duck,
clucking to herself in a terrible temper.
Suddenly Peter noticed a movement in the grass close by.
The cat was trying to sneak up and catch the bird!
"Look out!" called Peter as the cat suddenly leapt into
the air with his claws outstretched. He missed! The little
bird fluttered off and the cat slunk
crossly away. The duck clucked
angrily at the cat and the bird
for disturbing the peace and
Peter shrugged his shoulders
to see his three friends
so out of sorts with
one another.

Suddenly, Peter heard an angry shout. His grandfather was leaning over the garden gate. "Peter, come here!" he cried. "Haven't I told you to stay inside the garden? What if a wolf should come out of the wood and find you there?"

Peter hung his head. He was not afraid of some silly old wolf. But he did as his grandfather asked and walked back into the safety of the garden and closed the gate firmly behind him.

But just then, who should come out of the woods but a big grey wolf! The cat leapt up the tree at once. The bird sat on a branch and kept quite still. But down on the pond, the white duck panicked. If she had only stayed in the middle of the water she would have been safe, for wolves do not like to swim. But the poor duck was so afraid that she could not think straight. With a loud squawk she swam to the edge of the pond and scrambled onto the bank. The wolf was after her in a second. He reached her – he grabbed her – and he swallowed her!

Then the hungry wolf licked his lips. He had smelled something else interesting to eat! High in the tree the cat and the bird sat and trembled as the wolf slowly paced around the trunk and looked up at them with cruel yellow eyes.

Now Peter had seen everything that had happened and he knew at once what to do. He ran to the shed where his grandfather kept a strong rope. He coiled the rope about his shoulders and ran back outside.

He climbed up onto the high stone wall which ran around the garden and inched carefully along it, until he reached the place where the tree grew in the meadow on the other side of the wall. He could just reach one of the branches. He caught hold with both hands and swung himself up into the tree, as the wolf paced hungrily below him.

Then he whispered to the little bird. "You must help me with my plan," he said in a low voice. "Fly down from your branch and circle around the wolf's nose."
The little bird began to tremble and shake. "I will not be able to do that," she cheeped. "He will catch me in his strong jaws for sure." Peter smiled at her reassuringly. "You flew around the duck well enough earlier. You dodged her sharp beak very cleverly and I am sure you will escape the wolf."
So the little bird plucked up courage and prepared to fly down from her branch.

"Be brave," whispered Peter, "and be careful."
At first the wolf did not know what this strange thing was that darted about his head. Angrily he swiped at it with his large grey paw. But the bird was so quick and clever that the wolf missed her every time. Soon she had lost her fear and took great delight in teasing the frustrated wolf as he jumped this way and that.

While the little bird kept the wolf fully occupied, Peter was busy with his plan. He made a loop with his rope and slowly lowered it down from the branch until it hung just above the wolf's tail. There it dangled to and fro as the angry wolf snarled at the little bird.

Peter held his breath and waited for the right moment. Then, what joy! The wolf's tail flicked inside the loop and in a flash, Peter pulled the rope tight and he was caught. The wolf knew at once what had happened and what a rage he was in! Quickly Peter tied the other end of the rope around the tree trunk and then the old gray wolf was caught fast. Angrily he leapt up and down and tried to free himself, but the more he jumped, the tighter the rope pulled around his tail and held him firm. The little bird sang in triumph and Peter clapped his hands.

Just then two hunters crept from the wood with guns gripped firmly against their shoulders. They had been tracking the wolf and had followed him as far as the meadow.

"Don't shoot!" cried Peter. "The bird and I have caught the wolf. Please help us take him to the zoo."

Then Peter, the cat and the bird came down from the tree and explained all that had happened. Peter's grandfather shook his head in worry when he heard the news.

"But what if you had not caught the wolf?" he said. "What would have happened to you then?"

But Peter smiled bravely. "I had to help my friends," he said simply. The cat hissed and spat as the hunters cut the wolf down from the tree and tied him up.

Then Peter proudly led the procession across the meadow. And deep in the wolf's stomach the white duck still quacked crossly!

The Dog and His Reflection

There was once a naughty Dog. He was always hungry and no matter how large a meal he had to eat, he always found room for one or two bites more. His favorite shop was the Butcher's shop and he loved to sit outside and admire the strings of shiny sausages and rows of pink pork chops. How he wished he could help himself to something to eat! Come rain or shine, the Dog would sit happily all day long watching the Butcher at his work. But the Butcher did not like to see the Dog.

"Be off!" he would cry. "I have no meat for you!" Then the Dog would slink away with his tail between his legs.

One day the Dog woke up and looked at his empty cupboard in dismay. "Time to find some food," he said. Soon he was at the Butcher's, and there in the window was the most wonderful ham bone! The Dog sniffed longingly. He wanted that ham bone! As soon as the Butcher's back was turned, the Dog ran into the shop and seized the ham bone in his strong teeth. Off down the street he ran leaving the Butcher far behind him. The Butcher waved his sharpest knife and shouted after him angrily.

The Dog trotted along happily, feeling very pleased with himself.

"Nobody has a bone as big and as tasty as mine!" the Dog said to himself as he headed for home. He could hardly wait to start eating it.

But as he crossed the bridge over the stream
something caught his eye. There below him was
another Dog and this Dog was also
carrying a bone – and this bone was just as big
and tasty as his own! Angrily the Dog snarled over
the bridge. The other Dog snarled back.
The Dog was astonished.
"I shall have that bone," he decided. "Two bones
are better than one!" With that, the silly Dog
opened his mouth and snapped greedily at the
other bone.

But what a shock he got when his own bone tumbled from his mouth and landed with a splash in the water. To the Dog's great dismay the bone sank quickly out of sight and he realised he was left with nothing at all. He had been looking at his own reflection! Slowly he trudged back to his kennel, feeling very sorry for himself. He lay down and rested his head upon his paws. If only he had not been so greedy he would have a nice big bone to chew on now.
"I was wrong," sighed the Dog unhappily. "One bone is much, much better than none."

And the moral of this story is:
"Be grateful for what you have."

How the Leopard Got His Spots

Long ago, the Leopard and the Ethiopian lived in a 'sclusively bare, hot and sandy-yellow-brownish place called the High Veldt. The Giraffe and the Zebra lived there too and they were 'sclusively sandy-yellow-brownish all over. But not as sandy-yellow-brownish as the Leopard and the Ethiopian. The Leopard would hide behind a brownish rock and the Ethiopian would hide behind some yellowish grass and when the Giraffe or Zebra came by, they would leap out of their hiding places and give them the fright of their jumpsome lives. Indeed they would! After a while the Giraffe and the Zebra learned to stay away from places that could be hiding a Leopard or an Ethiopian and they began to look for somewhere else to live.

The Giraffe and the Zebra went to the forest. It was quite different from the High Veldt for it was full of stripy, speckly, patchy-blatchy shadows and there they hid safe from harm. After a long time, what with standing in the slippery-slidy shadows of the trees, the Giraffe grew blotchy and the Zebra grew stripy. By now the Leopard and the Ethiopian had grown very hungry and so they asked Baviaan, the wise Baboon, where the other animals had gone. "They decided it was high time for a change and they have gone into other spots and my advice to you, Leopard, is to do the same."

Then the Leopard and the Ethiopian searched the forest but although they could smell them and hear them, to their great surprise they found they could not see the animals.

Soon it grew dark, and the Leopard heard something breathing sniffily quite near him. It smelt like Zebra and when he stretched out his paw it felt like Zebra. So the Leopard jumped out of his tree and sat on this strange thing until morning because there was something about it that he didn't quite like. Presently he heard a grunt and a crash and he heard the Ethiopian call out. "I've caught a thing that I cannot see. It smells like Giraffe and it kicks like Giraffe but it hasn't any shape."

"Don't trust it," advised the Leopard. "Just sit on its head till the morning comes, same as me." So there they sat and waited until the sun rose, for then the light would show them just what they had caught.

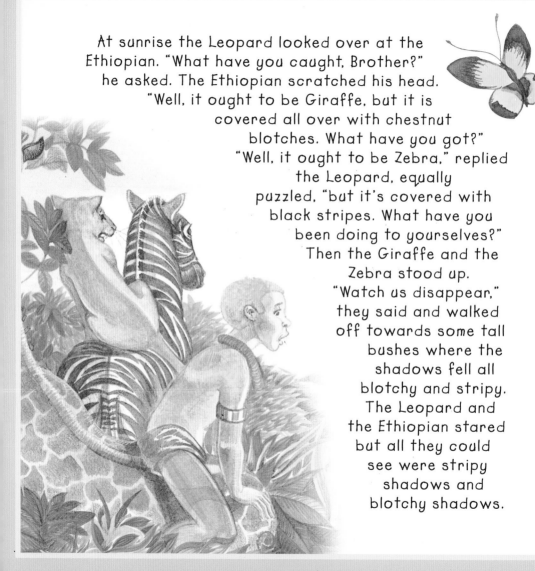

At sunrise the Leopard looked over at the Ethiopian. "What have you caught, Brother?" he asked. The Ethiopian scratched his head. "Well, it ought to be Giraffe, but it is covered all over with chestnut blotches. What have you got?" "Well, it ought to be Zebra," replied the Leopard, equally puzzled, "but it's covered with black stripes. What have you been doing to yourselves?" Then the Giraffe and the Zebra stood up. "Watch us disappear," they said and walked off towards some tall bushes where the shadows fell all blotchy and stripy. The Leopard and the Ethiopian stared but all they could see were stripy shadows and blotchy shadows.

"That's a lesson worth learning!" declared the Ethiopian. "I'm going to change myself, too. I want to be a nice blackish-brownish color. It will be the very thing for hiding in hollows and behind trees." So he changed his skin then and there and when he had finished he spoke to his friend. "You should take Baviaan's advice, Leopard, and go into other spots, too." "Very well," said the Leopard, "but don't make 'em too vulgar-big. I wouldn't look like Giraffe - not for ever so."

So the Ethiopian pressed his five fingers over the Leopard and they left five little black marks, all close together. Soon the Leopard was covered in spots. If you look closely at any Leopard now you will see that there are always five spots – off five fingertips.

"Now you can lie out on the ground and look like a heap of pebbles," said the Ethiopian. "You can lie on a leafy branch and look like dappled sunshine. Think of that and purr!" And so the animals were very proud of their new coats and were very glad that they had changed. Oh, one last thing. Now and again you will hear grown-ups say, "Can the Leopard change his spots?" I don't think even grown-ups would keep on saying such a silly thing if the Leopard hadn't done it once – do you? But he will never do it again, Best Beloved. Oh no, he is quite contented just as he is.

Three Billy Goats Gruff

Once upon a time in a land far away there lived three Billy Goats who were brothers.

There was a large Billy Goat, a middle-sized Billy Goat and a small Billy Goat. They were the Three Billy Goats Gruff. They lived high up on a rocky mountainside and leapt from peak to peak in search of food. But they found very little grass to eat and often went to sleep with their empty tummies rumbling with hunger.

"We will look for a better place to live," decided the oldest Billy Goat at last. "Somewhere with plenty of good, sweet grass to eat."

So the next day they set off in search of a new home. They climbed down the rocky mountainside, and soon they reached the valley far below.

"That is the place for us," said the oldest Billy Goat and he nodded his head at a lush green meadow on the other side of a swift mountain stream. Now the only way to cross that stream was over a rickety wooden bridge and under that rickety wooden bridge lived the ugliest, fiercest troll that ever was. He liked nothing better than to gobble up goats for his supper.

But the three Billy Goats Gruff were brave goats, and were not going to let that mean troll keep them from the lush green meadow.

So the smallest Billy Goat Gruff stamped his hoof and set off over the bridge, trip, trap, trip, trap. "Who's that trip-trapping over my bridge?" roared the troll and the little Billy Goat stood stock-still.

"It is me, the smallest Billy Goat Gruff,"
he said. "I am off to the meadow to
eat the sweet grass."
"Oh, no, you are not!" roared the troll,
"for I am going to eat you all up!"
"But I am small and bony," replied the
smallest Billy Goat. "You should wait for
my brother. He is much fatter than me."
The troll scratched his head and the
smallest Billy Goat Gruff quickly
trotted over the bridge and
was soon safe on the
other side.

Then the middle-sized Billy Goat Gruff began to cross the bridge. "Who is that trip-trapping over my bridge?" roared the ugly, fierce troll.

"It is me, the middle-sized Billy Goat Gruff and I am off to the meadow to eat the sweet grass," he said.

"Oh, no, you are not! I am going to gobble you up!" cried the troll and he reared up from his hiding place.

"You don't want to do that," replied the Billy Goat.
"You should wait for my big brother."
So the troll let the middle-sized Billy Goat pass by and
waited for the largest Billy Goat Gruff to appear.

Soon he came trotting over the bridge, trip, trap, trip, trap. "Who is that trip-trapping over my bridge?" roared the angry troll. "I am going to eat you all up!" But the biggest Billy Goat Gruff did not look at all afraid. He pawed the rickety wooden bridge with his strong hooves, lowered his head and then the troll suddenly spotted his two sharp horns – but it was too late! The big Billy Goat Gruff thundered towards him and his mighty horns butted the troll high into the air.

He landed in the river with a loud splash and was never seen again.

And the Three Billy Goats Gruff lived happily ever after in their lush meadow and grew very fat indeed!

⭐ The Fox and the Crow ⭐

There was once a fine Fox. He had a glossy red coat
and a beautiful bushy tail. His pointed ears pricked up
at the smallest sound and his sharp nose twitched at
the faintest smell.

Early one evening as the Fox prowled under the old oak trees, his black nose began to prickle. "What a wonderful smell!" said the Fox to himself. "It is better than rabbits. It is better than chickens. What could it be?" He bent his head to the ground and snuffled amongst the leaves and the grass. The tantalizing smell was not down there. He sniffed again. "Where is this marvelous smell coming from?" he puzzled. He raised his nose high in the air and sniffed once more. Then he caught sight of something perched high above him on the branch of an oak tree.

It was a glossy black crow and she was holding something in her beak. Something yellow. Something tasty. Something very like cheese! The Fox licked his lips. He badly wanted that piece of cheese. But how was he to reach it? He certainly could not jump high enough to catch the bird, and he could not climb the tree.

Then the cunning Fox had a clever idea. He looked up at the Crow and the Crow looked down at him. "What a magnificent bird!" exclaimed the Fox. "Such glossy black feathers. Such a bright yellow beak."

The Crow stood quite still but she quivered with pleasure to hear the Fox's charming words. "What sparkling eyes!" continued the Fox. "They glitter like two beads of jet. I cannot believe there is a bird anywhere in the world who could match this beautiful Crow."

The Crow had never heard such flattery and she fluffed up her feathers and bobbed up and down on the branch, drinking in the bold Fox's honeyed words. Then the Fox spoke again, and as he spoke his eyes never left the large piece of cheese.

"I wonder if the Crow's voice is as splendid as her appearance," he said. "She would indeed be Queen of all the Birds if such a wondrous bird was also blessed with a glorious singing voice."
Then the vain Crow could not resist the chance to show off and opening her beak wide, she began to caw loudly. Well, the wily Fox knew just what would happen next and he was waiting!

The cheese tumbled from the Crow's beak and fell straight into the Fox's open mouth. He chewed it slowly and lovingly and at last swallowed it with a happy sigh. "Very tasty," he said, and he licked his lips as the Crow screeched with rage above his head.

"Well," said the Fox smugly. "So you do have a voice. My, but what a pity it is that you were not blessed with a brain!" and he sauntered off with his tail held high in the air.

And the 'moral' of this story is:
Never trust a flatterer.

BRER RABBIT
AND
THE WELL

Brer Rabbit was hard at work in the garden with Brer Fox, Brer Raccoon and Brer Bear. The sun was hot and he was tired out and fed up. He didn't let on to the others that he was tired because he didn't want them to start saying he was lazy. No, siree. So he carried on pulling up the weeds until by and by he let out a yell. "Oo,oo! I gotta sharp thorn in my paw!" he cried, pretending he had hurt himself. Then off he skipped mighty quick to find a nice cool place to rest. Pretty soon he came across a well with a bucket hanging down into its shady depths.

"That sure looks cool," he said to himself. "That looks like the very spot for me," and into the bucket he jumped.

Well, the bucket didn't stay still! *No,* it dropped like a stone to the very bottom of the well. Poor Brer Rabbit didn't have much time to think about where he might be heading because all of a sudden the bucket hit the water with a loud splash and then Brer Rabbit knew that he was in a real fix. He hunched up tight and shivered as he wondered what might happen next.

Back in the meadow Brer Fox had stopped work. He always had one eye on what Brer Rabbit was up to and when he saw Brer Rabbit sneak off, he guessed he was up to no good and decided to follow him. He hid behind a tree and watched as Brer Rabbit stopped by the well, and when he saw him jump in the bucket he could hardly believe his eyes! "Well, if that isn't the darndest thing I ever did see," he muttered to himself.

Brer Fox sat and thought. "There has to be a mighty good reason why Brer Rabbit has gone down that well," he said to himself, and he thought some more. After a while he leapt up and cried, "I've got it! That must be where Brer Rabbit keeps all his money hidden! Or maybe he's found a gold mine!" He crept up to the well and peered over the edge. There wasn't a sound to be heard. Down at the bottom of the well poor Brer Rabbit sat hunched up in his bucket, hardly daring to twitch a whisker in case the bucket tipped him into the cold water. Suddenly a voice echoed down the well.

"Howdy, Brer Rabbit," called Brer Fox. "What are you doing down there?" Brer Rabbit thought hard.

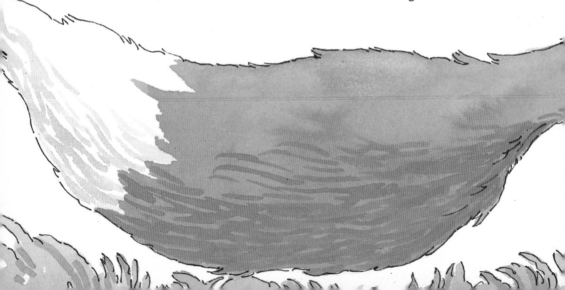

"I'm fishing," he replied. "There are some mighty fine fish down here, Brer Fox." Brer Fox licked his lips hungrily. He liked fish.
"Are there many fish down there, Brer Rabbit?" he asked.
"More than you or I could eat," said Brer Rabbit. Brer Fox strained his eyes in the darkness to catch a sight of those wonderful fish.
"Come on down and help me haul them in, Brer Fox. I could do with a hand," said Brer Rabbit. Brer Fox looked down into the dark shadows.
"I might just do that," he called out. "But how do I get down there? It's awful deep."
"That's easy," cried Brer Rabbit. "Just hop into that bucket you see at the top of the well and it'll bring you straight down for sure."

Well, Brer Fox could not resist the thought of all those fishes jumping and leaping and his stomach began to rumble. So he jumped into the bucket and down he went, down and down, heading for the bottom of the well.
But what he didn't realize was that as he went down, Brer Rabbit was going up!
The weight of the fox in the bucket was pulling the other bucket up to the top of the well.
Halfway down the well, they passed one another.
"Guess this is the way of the world, Brer Fox," laughed Brer Rabbit. "Some go up and some go down!" Then Brer Fox knew that Brer Rabbit had got the better of him and there was absolutely nothing he could do about it! Soon the bucket hit the water with a splash, and it was Brer Fox's turn to sit shivering in the darkness. "One of these days I'm going to teach that darned Rabbit a lesson," cursed Brer Fox.

When he reached the top of the well, Brer Rabbit hopped out of his bucket and ran straight to Brer Bear and Brer Raccoon.

"Brer Fox is down the well!" he cried, "and he's making our drinking water all muddy." The other animals were mighty mad at Brer Fox, and they headed straight for the well to find him. In no time at all they were hauling poor Brer Fox up and they hollered at him and boxed his ears for messing up their water! They wouldn't listen to his explanations and excuses. But that Brer Rabbit just hid behind a tree and watched as poor Brer Fox got in trouble, and he laughed and laughed to think how well he had tricked him!

GOLDILOCKS
& THE THREE BEARS

Once upon a time there were Three Bears. There was a large, gruff Father Bear, a middle-sized Mother Bear and a small, wee Baby Bear and they lived in a cottage in the middle of a wood.

One morning their porridge was too hot to eat, so the Three Bears decided to go for a walk while it cooled down. But when they were out who should come by but a little girl called Goldilocks. She peeked in the window and saw the porridge on the table. "Yummy!" she said. "I like porridge," and lifting the latch, she opened the door and walked inside.

Now Goldilocks was a naughty little girl, and did not wait to be invited to breakfast. She just sat down and helped herself!

First she tasted Father Bear's porridge, but that was much too salty. "Yuck!" said Goldilocks. Next she tasted Mother Bear's porridge, but that was too sweet.

"Disgusting!" said Goldilocks. So then she picked up Baby Bear's tiny spoon and tasted his porridge. It wasn't too salty and it wasn't too sweet. It was just right! In next to no time Baby Bear's bowl was empty.

Greedy Goldilocks had eaten the porridge all up!

Now she felt so full that she decided she must rest a while. First she tried Father Bear's chair. It had a flat wooden seat and a high back made of thin wooden spindles. Goldilocks sat down – but she soon scrambled off again. "What a horrid, hard chair!" she complained. Then she tried Mother Bear's chair. It was large and squishy and filled with fat feather cushions. "Goodness!" exclaimed Goldilocks. "Much too soft!"

Then she tried Baby Bear's little rocking chair. Father Bear had carved garden flowers into the oak wood. Goldilocks sat down. It wasn't too hard and it wasn't too soft. It was just right! "Perfect!" sighed Goldilocks happily, and with a tummy full of porridge and a big smile on her face, she leaned back and made herself comfortable. But she was too big and too heavy for Baby Bear's little chair and with a creak and a crash it broke into tiny pieces. Goldilocks was cross!

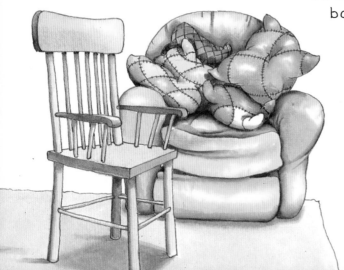

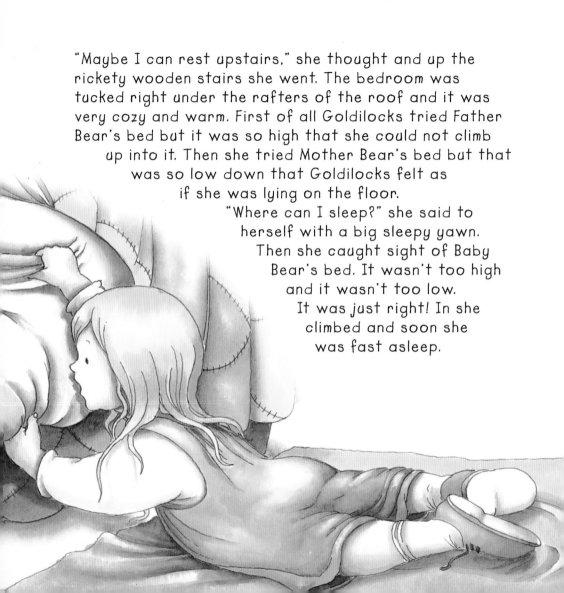

"Maybe I can rest upstairs," she thought and up the rickety wooden stairs she went. The bedroom was tucked right under the rafters of the roof and it was very cozy and warm. First of all Goldilocks tried Father Bear's bed but it was so high that she could not climb up into it. Then she tried Mother Bear's bed but that was so low down that Goldilocks felt as if she was lying on the floor.

"Where can I sleep?" she said to herself with a big sleepy yawn. Then she caught sight of Baby Bear's bed. It wasn't too high and it wasn't too low. It was just right! In she climbed and soon she was fast asleep.

After a while the Three Bears arrived back from their walk. They sat down at the table with rumbling tummies for they were very hungry, but they soon saw that something was wrong.

"Someone's been eating my porridge!" roared Father Bear and he looked very cross indeed.

"Someone's been eating my porridge!" growled Mother Bear. Then little Baby Bear looked at his plate.

"Someone's been eating my porridge," he squeaked, "and they've eaten it all up!"

They noticed that their chairs had been moved.

"Someone's been sitting in my chair!" said Father Bear.

"Someone's been sitting in my chair!" bellowed Mother Bear. Then little Baby Bear looked at his chair.

"Someone's been sitting in my chair!" he wailed, "and they've broken it into tiny pieces!"

"Whoever has done it must be hiding upstairs!" whispered Father Bear, and up the rickety wooden stairs they tiptoed, one behind the other.

"Someone's been sleeping in my bed!" grumbled Father Bear.

"Someone's been sleeping in my bed!" rumbled Mother Bear.

Then little Baby Bear looked at his bed. "Someone's been sleeping in my bed!" he squealed, "and she's still there!"

Then Goldilocks woke up with a start and when she saw the Three Bears looking so cross she jumped out of bed and ran like the wind down the rickety wooden stairs. Out of the door she flew and she didn't stop running until she was far away from the little cottage and the Three Bears – and after that they never saw Goldilocks again!

The Cat that Walked by Himself

Hear and attend; for this befell and behappened, O Best Beloved, when the Tame animals were wild. The Dog was wild, and the Horse was wild, and the Cow was wild, and the Sheep was wild, and the Pig was wild – as wild as wild could be – and they all walked in the Wet Wild Woods by their wild lones. But the wildest of all the wild animals was the Cat. He walked by himself and all places were alike to him.

Of course the Man was wild too. He was dreadfully wild. He didn't even begin to be tame till he met the Woman, and she told him that she did not like living in his wild ways. So she found a nice dry cave to lie down in and she lit a nice fire of wood at the back of the cave. Then she hung a dried wild-horse skin across the opening of the cave, and she said, "Wipe your feet, dear, when you come in, and now we'll keep house."

That night as the Man slept by the fire, the Woman sat up combing her hair. She took the bone of a shoulder of mutton and she looked at the wonderful marks that were carved on it and she made the First Singing Magic in the world. Out in the Wet Wild Woods the wild animals could see the bright light of the fire and they wondered what it meant. Wild Dog lifted up his head and said, "I will go up and see and look. Cat, come with me."

"No!" said the Cat. "I am the Cat who walks by himself, and all places are alike to me. I will not come." But the Cat secretly followed and hid himself where he could see and hear everything.

Wild Dog entered the cave and sniffed the beautiful smell of roast mutton and the Woman laughed. "Here comes the first Wild Thing out of the Wild Woods, what do you want?"

Wild Dog said, "Wife of my Enemy, what smells so good?" The Woman gave him the bone to gnaw and it was so delicious that he wanted another. "Wild Thing," said the Woman. "Help my Man to hunt and guard this cave at night, and I will give you as many bones as you need." And so the Wild Dog became the First Friend. "Ah!" said the Cat. "This is a wise Woman, but she is not so wise as I am." The next night the Woman made a Second Magic and this time the Wild Horse went to see the strange light. The Cat followed softly and watched him enter the cave.

The Woman said, "Here comes the second Wild Thing, what do you want?" The Wild Horse looked at the sweet grass on the floor of the cave. "Bend your head and wear this halter," said the Woman, "and you shall eat the grass three times a day."
"Ah!" said the Cat. "This is a clever Woman, but she is not so clever as I am."

When the Man and the Dog came back from hunting, the Woman said, "Wild Horse is now the First Servant and will carry us from place to place for always."
The next day the Woman made her Third Magic and this time the Wild Cow came up to the cave and she promised to give her milk to the Woman every day in return for the wonderful grass.

The Cat went back through the Wet Wild Woods and he never told anybody what he had seen. But in the morning he went back to the cave and he saw the light of the fire and he smelled the warm milk.

Then the Woman laughed and said, "Wild Thing out of the Wild Woods, go away for I have put away the magic bone, and we have no more need of either friends or servants in our cave."
Cat said, "I am not a friend, and I am not a servant. I am the Cat who walks by himself, and I wish to come in."

"No," said the Woman. "If you are the Cat who walks by himself, all places are alike to you. Go away and walk by yourself in all places alike." But the Cat liked the warm cave and he spoke again. "You are very wise and beautiful," he said. "You should not be cruel, even to a Cat." Then the Woman laughed.

"I knew I was wise, but I did not know I was beautiful. I will make a bargain with you. If ever I say one word in your praise, you may come into the cave. If ever I say two words in your praise, you may sit by the fire. And if ever I say three words in your praise, you may drink the warm milk for always."

Cat went far away and hid himself in the Wet Wild Woods for a long time till the Woman forgot all about him. Only the Bat that hung upside down in the cave knew where the Cat had hidden himself and one day he brought news.

"There is a Baby in the cave. He is new and pink and fat and small, and the Woman is very fond of him."
The next morning the Cat found the Baby sitting outside the cave. The Woman was busy cooking but the Baby's cries kept interrupting her. Then the Cat put out his paddy paw and patted the Baby on the cheek and the Baby laughed.

The Woman heard him and smiled.
"A blessing on that Wild Thing who is playing with my Baby," she said. "I am very busy and whoever he is, he is helping me by keeping the Baby happy."
Then the curtain fell down at the mouth of the cave and the Cat strolled inside and sat down.

The Woman was very angry to see the Cat inside the cave but she knew that the bargain had to be kept. The Baby began to cry once more and this time the Cat purred a gentle lullaby in its ear until it fell asleep.

"You are certainly very clever, O Cat," said the Woman.
Then the smoke suddenly puffed up from the fire and when it had cleared, there sat the Cat sitting quite comfy close to the heat of the flames.

"Now I can sit by the warm fire for always," said the Cat, "but still I am the Cat who walks by himself, and all places are alike to me." But the Woman was angry and promised herself she would not say a third word in praise of the Cat.

By and by the cave grew
so still that a little mouse
crept out of a corner and
ran across the floor.
"Ouh! Chee!" cried the
Woman, and she *jumped*
upon a stool. Then the
Cat made one pounce and
caught the little mouse in
his claws.
"A hundred thanks," said
the Woman. "You must be
very wise to catch a
mouse so easily." Then the
Milk-pot crackled in two
pieces and lo and behold!
the Cat was lapping up
the warm white milk!

That evening the Man and the Dog were not pleased to see the Cat in their cave. The Man took off his two leather boots and he set them in a row with his stone axe, a piece of wood and a hatchet.

"This is our bargain," he said. "If you do not catch mice in the cave for always, I will throw these things at you whenever I see you, and so shall all proper men do after me."

"And if you are not kind to the Baby," added the Dog, "then I will hunt you and try to bite you. And so shall all proper Dogs do after me."
But the Cat was not worried. "Still I am the Cat who walks by himself, and all places are alike to me."
Then the Man and the Dog were angry and they chased him up a tree. And from that moment to this three proper men out of five will always throw things at a Cat, and all proper Dogs will chase him.
But between times, and when the moon gets up and night comes, he is the Cat that walks by himself, and all places are alike to him.

⭐ The Town Mouse ⭐ and the Country Mouse

Once upon a time there were two little mice. They were cousins, but even though they came from the same family, each small mouse was very different from the other one.
One mouse was very grand and lived in the town in a fine house with a butler and maids. His rooms were lined with silk and richly colored carpets.

He slept on a duck-down mattress under a velvet cover. He wore a beautiful embroidered waistcoat and carried a silver-topped cane. Twirling his waxed moustache as he strolled along, he could never pass a mirror or shop window without first stopping to admire himself. He ate the best of foods and drank the finest wines. "What a lucky fellow I am!" the Town Mouse thought happily to himself.

His cousin lived in the country and was a very simple fellow. He lived under the roots of an old oak tree in a small hole lined with straw and dry grass. His floor was covered with crumbling oak leaves. He slept on an old scrap of sheep's wool that he had found clinging to a rusty nail on the farmer's fence. He wore a shabby brown waistcoat he had made himself from an old grainsack and he carried a long crooked stick with a hooked handle which he had carved himself from a twisted stick he had found in the woods.

He had never seen a mirror or a shop window in his life. He ate what food he could find in the hedgerows and used his stick to knock blackberries from the bushes hanging overhead.

"What a lucky fellow I am," the Country Mouse said to himself, with a smile.

One fine autumn day the Country Mouse decided he would like to share his happiness with his city cousin. "I must invite my cousin to come and stay in my cozy home," he said to himself, and busily started to prepare for the visit.

When the smart Town Mouse arrived he knocked loudly at the door.

"Welcome to my humble home," said the Country Mouse, helping his cousin off with his best silk coat.

The Town Mouse
looked about the
little hole in dismay.
What a shabby home!
"My dear chap!" he
exclaimed. "How can
you possibly live like
this?" He pointed at
the sheep's wool bed.
"You can't expect me
to sleep on that
smelly old pile
of fluff!"
"But it's warm and
dry," replied his
cousin. "What more
would you want?"

The Town Mouse looked at him in amazement, but before he could speak, the Country Mouse led him to a table piled high with food.

"I have prepared a special meal," he said excitedly. "A cob of corn, fresh hazelnuts, rosy red rosehips, and wild blackberry juice."

The Town Mouse wrinkled his nose in disgust, but nibbled politely at the juicy corn. "What dreadful food!" he thought, and dabbed his whiskers with a silk handkerchief.

Outside the full moon shone brightly and the owls hooted softly in the old oak tree.

All was peaceful.

"Time for bed," said the Country Mouse.

All night long the Town Mouse tossed and turned on his uncomfortable bed. "I can't sleep!" he complained. "It's just too quiet!"

The next morning his mind was made up.
"I am sorry, cousin," he said. "The dull country life is
not for me. Come and visit the town and see what
you are missing."
So the next day the Country Mouse returned with the
Town Mouse to his home in the big, busy city. Loud honks
and screeches filled the air.

"What kind of fierce animal is that?" asked the Country Mouse. "That is the sound of the traffic,' laughed the Town Mouse. "You will have to be careful when you cross the road!"

In and out of the speeding wheels they dodged until at last they arrived breathless on the far pavement. "This is terrible!" gasped the Country Mouse. "I have never been so scared in all my life!" "You will feel safer inside," said his cousin, guiding him towards a grand house behind tall iron railings.

"This is what a home should be like," said the Town Mouse proudly as he led the Country Mouse from room to room. "I like soft carpets and comfortable furniture. There are no leaves or mud here."

The Country Mouse could not believe his eyes. Never had he seen such beautiful furniture. Never had he stroked such soft silks. Never had he smelled such delicious smells!

"Come and eat," said the Town Mouse, "but there will be no rosehips or hazlenuts on the menu!" he added with a twinkle in his eye. They scampered into the dining room and onto the table. The little Country Mouse gasped when he saw the wonderful spread of food laid out. Large yellow cheeses, a whole leg of ham, mountains of fruit and a huge chocolate cake!

"This is real food," cried the Town Mouse. "Let us begin!" But just then two huge dogs came bounding into the room, barking fiercely. The two little mice raced through a hole in the skirting board, with the dogs' sharp teeth snapping behind them.

Panting for breath, and shaking like a leaf, the Country Mouse turned to his cousin.

"I'm going home!" he squeaked. "You may wear a velvet coat while my clothes are patched and darned. You may feast on roast beef and chocolate cake while I live on nuts and berries. You may sleep on a soft duck-down mattress while I have only a scrap of wool for my bed, but at least I can sleep safely at night. You can enjoy the excitement of the town if you wish, but give me the plain and simple life any time!"

And the moral of this story is: "Better a poor and carefree life than a rich and worried one."

The Golden Goose

Once upon a time there were three brothers. The youngest son was given the name of Dummling and was laughed at by his family and everyone else.

One day the eldest son went into the forest to cut some wood. His mother gave him cake and a bottle of wine and off he went, whistling cheerfully. But he had no sooner set to work than a little old man appeared. "I am so hungry and thirsty. May I have some cake and wine?" asked the old man. But the eldest son shook his head.

"Be off with you," he said gruffly. "I will share my meal with no one." But it seemed the old man was going to get his revenge, as the very next swing of the selfish boy's axe landed on his very own foot. How he yelled!

The next day the second son decided to try his luck and once again his mother gave him cake and wine.

The little old man approached the second son and asked to share his meal, but the second son also refused. He, too, was cut by the next swing of his axe.

The next day Dummling set off for the forest to cut some wood. He was given only bread and water but was happy to share what he had with the little man.

"You are a good boy," said the man, "and if you cut down that tree you will get your reward." Dummling did as he was bid and was astonished to find a goose covered with golden feathers.

"I will go to the city and seek my fortune," Dummling decided. "This beautiful goose will bring me luck."

As he strolled along the lane he passed a girl.
She gasped to see such a beautiful golden bird and
stretched out her hand to stroke it. But imagine her dismay
when she found that she could not take her hand away!
The goose had magic powers and whoever laid a finger
on her soon found themselves stuck fast to her feathers.
Before long, Dummling had collected two more curious
girls and a Parson, all stuck fast one behind the other. As
they stumbled across the fields they met the Bishop.
"My dear Parson!" he cried. "Have you taken leave of
your senses?" and he reached out and caught the
Parson's sleeve. Now he, too, was stuck fast and it
wasn't long before they were joined by a ploughman
and a shepherd!

After a time they reached the city and there in the
palace lived the King and his daughter. She had never
been known to smile and the King had promised her hand
in marriage to the first person who was able to make
her laugh. Well, when the Princess saw the three girls,
the Parson, the Bishop, the ploughman and the poor
shepherd all falling over one another behind Dummling's
golden Goose, she burst into peals of laughter.
The King came running and Dummling lost no time in asking
his permission to marry the Princess.
"Hmm," thought the King to himself. "I do not want this
raggle taggle boy to marry my daughter. I must set
him an impossible task to perform and when he
fails, I will be able to refuse him."

And so the King told Dummling that before the marriage could take place he would first have to find a man who could drink a whole cellarful of wine.

Dummling scratched his head and then he remembered the old man in the forest. But when he returned to the glade the old man was not there. Instead, he found a short man with a miserable face.

"Oh, my, I am so terribly thirsty," he moaned. "I have already drunk a barrel of wine but I feel as if I could drain a lake dry!"

"You are just the man I am looking for!" cried Dummling and he led the man to the King's cellar.

The fat man rubbed his hands with glee. "This is a sight for sore eyes!" the short man declared and soon he had emptied every bottle, keg, cask and barrel.

The King was amazed. He decided to set another even harder task.

"Find me a man who can eat a whole mountain of bread," he ordered, certain that this would be impossible. But Dummling went straight to the forest and found a tall, thin man sitting on a log.

"I have just had four ovenfuls of bread for my supper but it has barely taken the edge of my appetite," he complained.

"I know a place where you can eat your fill," Dummling said. When he arrived back at the Palace the cooks set to work and baked enough bread to fill the whole courtyard! The tall, thin man ate and ate and ate and within hours the mountain had become a molehill, and soon there was nothing left at all.

Then the King set one last impossible task. "Find me a ship which can sail both on land and on sea. Only then can you marry my daughter," he declared.

This time Dummling found the little old man waiting for him in the forest. "I have not forgotten your kindness," he said. "Now look behind you." Then, with a great gust of wind filling its sails, the most magnificent ship sailed into the glade. When the King saw the ship sailing over the fields towards his palace he knew he would have to give in and so Dummling and the Princess were married.

They lived happily ever after but back at home Dummling's two brothers grew bitter and miserable — and all for the lack of a good, generous heart.

BRER RABBIT
AND THE
PEANUT PATCH

Brer Fox wasn't much of a gardener; ask anybody,
they'll all tell you the same thing. But one year he
decided it was high time he got the hang of growing
things and he decided he would plant a peanut patch.
Well, once he'd made his mind up to do it he was
raring to go.

"I'm going to plant me some peanuts," he declared to
the world, and the words were hardly out of his mouth
before the ground was freshly dug over and those
peanut plants were firmly in place. Brer Fox was
mighty proud of his peanut patch. He weeded it and
watered it and looked forward very much to the
day when he could eat a fine crop of nuts. But
Brer Rabbit had his eye on that self same
peanut patch and one morning, when the
peanuts had grown big and ripe, he crept
through the fence and helped himself
just as sassy as you please.

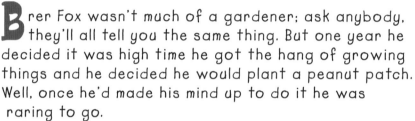

Every morning Brer Fox went down to his peanut patch to inspect his crop and when he saw that somebody had been scrabbling in and out of his plants he grew mighty mad. He looked after those little plants like his own children and he felt mighty protective of them.

Now Brer Fox had his suspicions about just who it might be that was sneaking into his peanut patch. And when he found a small hole in the fence around his garden he thought of a way he could soon find out for sure.

"I'm going to make a trap and catch that no-good varmint who's stealing my peanuts if it's the last thing I do," he said to himself. Soon he had made a fine trap with some rope and a slim hickory sapling and he positioned it right next to the hole in the fence.

The very next day Brer Rabbit came sashaying down the road towards the peanut patch. When he reached Brer Fox's fence, he bent down and wriggled all unsuspecting through the hole. What a fright he got when he suddenly found himself whisked up in the air and dangling by his back paws on the end of a rope! There he swung, to and fro, feeling mighty scared, and trying his best to think of a way out of this tricky situation.

Just then Brer Bear came ambling down the road.

"Howdy, Brer Bear!" called Brer Rabbit, just as cool and calm as he could. Brer Bear's huge head slowly turned from side to side.

"I'm up here!" called Brer Rabbit.

"What in tarnation are you doin' up there?" asked the astonished Bear as he looked up to see Brer Rabbit hanging upside down above him.

Brer Rabbit smiled at him in an upside down sort of a way. "Why, I'm earning a dollar a minute guarding the peanut patch for Brer Fox," replied the crafty Rabbit. "All I have to do is keep the crows out." "A dollar a minute!" spluttered Brer Bear. "That's pretty good going, Brer Rabbit."

"Sure is," said Brer Rabbit. "But I reckon I've earned enough money now. I don't suppose you want to take over from me?" Brer Bear looked at him doubtfully. "Do you reckon I could do it?" he asked. Brer Rabbit nodded encouragingly. "Why, it's easy as pie," he said. "I reckon you were born to be a scarecrow. I'll show you what to do!"

Soon Brer Rabbit was freed and standing safely on the ground and Brer Bear was hanging in his place in the tree. Brer Rabbit looked mighty happy to be down on the ground once again. He jumped in the air then raced off to Brer Fox's house, leaving poor Brer Bear swinging in the breeze.

"Brer Fox, come out!" shouted the naughty Rabbit. "I'll show you the rascal who's been stealing your peanuts!" Out shot Brer Fox with a big stick in his hand, and up the road they both ran, lickety-split.

"So that's your game, is it?" shouted Brer Fox when he found Brer Bear hanging from the tree, and he set about poor Brer Bear with his stick. Brer Bear tried to explain that he was guarding his peanut patch for him but the furious Brer Fox did not believe a word of it. And where was Brer Rabbit? Why, he was long gone. Long gone!

Puss in Boots

There was once an old miller who died, and left a will dividing his property between his three sons. He gave his eldest son his mill, his second son his donkey, and his youngest son his cat. The youngest son was unhappy to be left such a small share, and complained that his brothers could make a living from their inheritance, but a cat was only good for catching mice. He was worried that he would starve to death.

But the cat spoke gravely to his new master and told him not to worry. He asked for a bag and a pair of boots, promising to prove he was the best inheritance the boy could wish for.

The youngest son decided to give the cat a chance, and with the last of his money bought a bag, a hat and a smart new pair of boots for the cat.

The first thing the cat did was to fill his new bag with thistles, and set off for the rabbit warren. Before long he had caught a young rabbit, and at once he headed for the Palace, where he asked to see the King. "I have brought you a gift from my noble Lord, the Marquis of Carabas." (for that was the name which Puss had made up for his new master.) "We hope your Royal Majesty will enjoy it."

The King was most impressed by this elegant cat and his charming speech. He told the cat to thank his master for his most pleasing gift.

A few days later the cat caught some partridges, and once again presented them to the King. "From my noble Lord, the Marquis of Carabas," he said.

Over the next few months the cat visited the King often with many gifts from the Marquis of Carabas, and the King was intrigued and delighted.

Then one day Puss heard that the King was to take a drive by the river with his beautiful daughter, the Princess. The clever cat hurried to his master and told him, "Do as I say and your fortune will be made."

So the young man went to the river, as the cat had told him, undressed, and got in to bathe. Soon the King passed by in his coach, and Puss began to cry out: "Help! My Lord Marquis of Carabas is drowning!" Hearing the commotion, the King looked through his window and saw the cat who had brought him gifts.

The King commanded his footmen to help the Marquis.

Now, Puss had hidden his master's clothes, but told the King that they had been stolen. So after pulling the Marquis from the river, the footmen ran to the castle to fetch him some new clothes from the King's own wardrobe. And so it was that clever Puss made sure his master met the beautiful Princess looking very fine and impressive indeed. She thought he was the most handsome man she had ever seen, and he was just as taken with her. The King invited the Marquis to join them, and soon he was sitting next to the lovely Princess. Puss was delighted to see his plan working. He ran ahead of the coach and soon reached some mowers working in a meadow.

Scowling fiercely at them, he made them promise that when the King passed by they would tell him the meadow belonged to the Marquis of Carabas. They were frightened by the threats that Puss had made, so when the King arrived they told him the fine field belonged to the Marquis of Carabas, as Puss had told them. The King was most impressed and congratulated the Marquis. Meanwhile, Puss had run ahead to the cornfield, and threatened the workers there in the same way. When the King arrived at the cornfield, he was again told that it belonged to the Marquis of Carabas. Most impressed, he congratulated him again. And thus their journey continued. Puss ran ahead and warned each person he met to tell the King the same story. Before long, the King was quite astonished by the vast estates of the Marquis of Carabas.

Soon Puss came to a magnificent castle, which he had discovered belonged to a terrible ogre. The ogre was very rich and owned all of the land through which the King had been driven. Fearlessly, Puss strode up to the castle door and knocked loudly. The ogre was surprised by his visitor, but Puss soon charmed him with flattering words, and the ogre invited him inside.

"I have heard," said Puss, "that you have magic powers, and can change yourself into any creature you want. Is it true?"

"Indeed it is," said the ogre, proudly, "and if you don't believe me, watch this!" With a loud bang and a flash, there stood a huge lion, roaring fiercely! Puss was terrified, but in an instant, the ogre changed back again.

"Amazing!" said Puss. "But I bet you couldn't change into something small like a mouse !"

"Oh, couldn't I?" said the ogre, feeling insulted. "Watch this!"

With a flash and a bang he changed into a mouse and ran about the floor. In an instant, Puss pounced and gobbled him up! And so, with the ogre gone for good, Puss had won a castle, lands and vast riches for his master.

When the King's coach arrived, Puss bowed and said, "Your Majesty is most welcome to the home of my lord Marquis of Carabas." The King was amazed, and eagerly led the way into the castle. Inside they found a splendid banquet waiting (for the ogre had eaten well!). Puss served food and wine, and the Marquis behaved as if he had always been a noble Lord!

The King was most impressed by all he had seen, and could tell that the Princess had fallen in love, so he offered the Marquis his daughter's hand in marriage. They were overjoyed, and married the very next day. As for Puss, he was delighted his plan had worked. He was made a noble Lord, and never had to catch mice again — well, only for fun!

The Fox and the Stork

One day a Fox decided to invite a Stork to tea. He made all the preparations in the kitchen and set the table with his best crockery. He brushed his fine long tail until it shone like copper and then dressed in his best blue coat. Soon there was a tap, tap, tap upon the door. It was the Stork and with a great flourish, the Fox opened the door and bowed low.

"Do step inside," he cried. "Welcome to my humble home."

The Stork looked very elegant in a beautiful purple hat and matching cape and as she stepped daintily into the room her hat feathers quivered. She was very hungry. "I do hope the Fox has plenty of food," she said to herself anxiously.

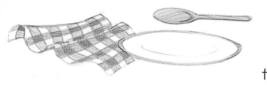

"I have cooked some beautiful soup," announced the Fox. "Let us begin," and he showed the Stork to a chair.

But the poor Stork was dismayed to see that the only plates laid upon the table were quite flat. How would she be able to eat soup from such a dish?

The Fox came bustling in from the kitchen and carefully set a steaming pot of soup down on the table.

The Fox ladled out the soup with much smacking of lips and many appreciative sniffs. Then he sat down, lifted his spoon and smiled broadly at the Stork.

"Do tuck in!" he urged. "This is my best soup!"

But the Stork looked down at her plate and sighed unhappily. She could not swallow this soup with her long pointed beak and so she could only sit and watch as the Fox greedily lapped up his plateful.

When the Fox had quite finished he looked across at the Stork in surprise.

"Did you not enjoy the soup?" he asked, wrinkling his brow as if greatly concerned. But the poor Stork was too polite to complain and so the wily Fox lapped up her portion as well.

The next day when the Stork awoke she was still hungry. She decided to repay the Fox's hospitality and invited him to dinner that evening. He was delighted and accepted eagerly.

But as the Fox sat down to eat at the Stork's table he could hardly believe his eyes. The only dishes upon the table were two tall jugs! The Stork dipped her slender beak inside the jug and drank her soup but the Fox could only lick his lips hungrily and watch, for there was no way he could get at the food.

He returned home a wiser Fox with nobody to blame but himself for, as he plainly realized, he had only been paid back for his own uncaring behavior.

And the 'moral' of this story is: Do as you would be done by.

★ The Elephant's Child ★

In the High and Far-Off Times the Elephant had no trunk. He had only a blackish, bulgy nose, as big as a boot, that he could wriggle about from side to side, but he couldn't pick things up with it.

Now there was one Elephant, a new Elephant, an Elephant's Child, who was full of 'satiable curiosity – and that means he asked ever so many questions. And he lived in Africa and he filled all Africa with his 'satiable curiosities.

He asked his tall aunt, the Ostrich, why her tail-feathers grew just so. He asked his tall uncle, the Giraffe, what made his skin spotty. He asked his broad aunt, the Hippopotamus, why her eyes were red and he asked his hairy uncle, the Baboon, why melons tasted just so. He asked questions about everything that he saw, or heard, or felt, or smelled, or touched, and his aunts and his uncles spanked him but still he was full of 'satiable curiosity!

One fine morning the Elephant's Child asked a fine new question that he had never asked before. "What does the Crocodile have for dinner?" he said. Then everybody said, "Hush!" and spanked him again. When they had quite finished, the Elephant's Child came upon a Kolokolo Bird sitting in a thorn bush.

"If you want to find out what the Crocodile has for dinner," said the Bird, "you must go to the banks of the great grey-green, greasy Limpopo River, all set about with fever-trees, and there you will find out." So the Elephant's Child set off to find the Crocodile.

Now you must understand, O Best
Beloved, that this 'satiable Elephant's
Child had never seen a Crocodile,
and did not know what one was
like. But nevertheless he set off
for the Limpopo River and the
first thing that he found was
a Bi-Colored-Python-
Rock-Snake curled
round a rock.

"'Scuse me," said the Elephant's Child most politely, "but have you seen such a thing as a Crocodile in these promiscuous parts?" Then the Bi-Colored-Python-Rock-Snake uncoiled himself very quickly from the rock, and spanked the Elephant's Child with his scalesome, flailsome tail, and when he had finished the Elephant's Child thanked him politely and continued on his way.

After a while he trod on what he thought was a log of wood at the edge of the great Limpopo River, but it was really the Crocodile, who winked one eye. "'Scuse me," said the Elephant's Child most politely, "but do you happen to have seen a Crocodile in these promiscuous parts?" Then the Crocodile winked the other eye, and lifted half his tail out of the mud, and the Elephant's Child stepped back as he did not wish to be spanked again.

"Come hither, Little One," said the Crocodile. "Why do you ask such things?" "'Scuse me," said the Elephant's Child, "but all my aunts and uncles have spanked me and the Bi-Colored-Python-Rock-Snake has spanked me and so, if it's all the same to you, I don't want to be spanked again."

"Come hither, Little One," said the Crocodile, "for I am the Crocodile," and he wept crocodile tears to show it was quite true. "You are the very person I have been looking for all these long days," said the Elephant's Child. "Will you please tell me what you have for dinner?"

"Come hither, Little One," said the Crocodile, "and I'll whisper." So the Elephant's Child bent his head down close to the Crocodile's musky, tusky mouth, and the Crocodile caught him by his little nose, which up to that moment had been no bigger than a boot.

"I think," said the Crocodile from between his teeth, "I think today I will begin with Elephant's Child!" and he pulled and he pulled and he pulled.

"Led go!" cried the Elephant's Child. "You are hurting me!"

Then the Bi-Colored-Python-Rock-Snake scuffled down the bank and knotted himself in a double-clove-hitch around the Elephant's Child's legs. And he pulled, and the Elephant's Child pulled, and the Crocodile pulled – but the Elephant's Child and the Bi-Colored-Python-Rock-Snake pulled hardest (and by this time the poor nose was nearly five feet long!) At last the Crocodile let go of the Elephant's Child's nose with a plop that you could hear all up and down the Limpopo. Then the Elephant's child dangled his poor pulled nose in the water. "I am waiting for it to shrink," he explained.

There he sat for three days patiently waiting for his nose to shrink back to its usual size but the long stretched nose never grew any shorter. For the Crocodile had pulled it out into a really truly trunk same as all Elephants have today.

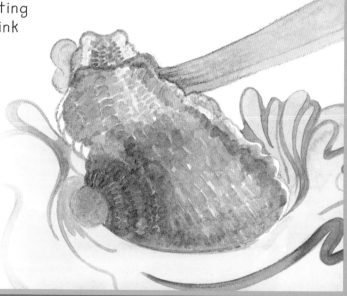

At the end of
the third day a
fly came and stung him on
the shoulder and before
he knew what he was
doing he lifted up his
trunk and hit that fly
dead. Later he grew
hungry, so almost without
thinking he put out his
trunk and plucked a large
bundle of grass and
stuffed it in his mouth.

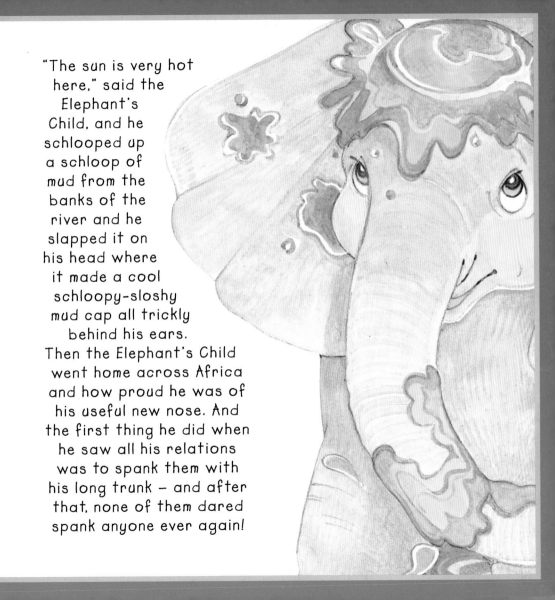

"The sun is very hot here," said the Elephant's Child, and he schlooped up a schloop of mud from the banks of the river and he slapped it on his head where it made a cool schloopy-sloshy mud cap all trickly behind his ears. Then the Elephant's Child went home across Africa and how proud he was of his useful new nose. And the first thing he did when he saw all his relations was to spank them with his long trunk – and after that, none of them dared spank anyone ever again!

HOW MISS COW WAS MILKED

Late one afternoon Brer Rabbit was on his way home after a good day rooting about in Brer Fox's peanut patch. As the long shadows stretched out across the dusty ground he stopped and yawned. "I sure could do with something to drink," he said to himself.

Just then he spied Miss Cow grazing peacefully in the meadow. He would love a drink of milk, but he knew that Miss Cow would not give him some. No, siree. He had asked once before and she had sent him on his way with a toss of her horns. So he would just have to think of a plan.

"Howdy, Sis Cow," he said, as he leaned over the fence. "Why howdy, Brer Rabbit," replied Miss Cow and she carried on chewing the sweet grass.

"How's life treating you these days, Sis Cow?" said Brer Rabbit, all polite and respectful.

"Just fine, thank you," replied Miss Cow, gazing at him with her big brown eyes. "And how's life treating you?"

"No complaints," said Brer Rabbit, smiling sweetly.

"Could you do me a little favor, Sis Cow?" Brer Rabbit went on, all big eyes and innocence. Miss Cow stopped chewing and looked up at him. "I see there are some mighty fine persimmons in that there tree. I sure would like to taste some of that fruit," said Brer Rabbit, pointing to a large tree growing in the meadow. "If you shake the trunk, then they will fall down off the branches and we can share them."

Now Miss Cow was a friendly creature and all too happy to oblige. She ran at the tree and banged her horns hard against the trunk – BLAM! But not one fruit fell down. Then Miss Cow took several steps backwards, lowered her head and ran at the tree at full speed – BLIM! Not one fruit moved from the branch, and it was no wonder, as they were as green as grass and nowhere near ripe enough to fall – as Brer Rabbit knew full well. Then Miss Cow backed up again. This time she hit the tree so hard that it was a wonder she didn't knock herself out on the spot. But what a shock she had when she came to step away from the tree and found that she couldn't move! One of her horns was stuck in the trunk! Brer Rabbit smiled to himself for his plan had worked perfectly.

Off ran that wily Brer Rabbit and pretty soon he was back with all his little children and each one carried a clanking milk pail! The children clustered so tight around Miss Cow that you could hardly see her and right in the very center of them sat Brer Rabbit on a three legged stool, milking away for all he was worth. He filled pail after pail with the sweet warm milk and pretty soon he had milked Miss Cow dry. When he was done he tipped his hat politely.

"I realized you might be stuck there all night and figured that you'd be pretty sore carrying all that milk, so I thought I'd help you out. Kind of a good deed, you might say," and with that he set off for home, with all his children following behind him carrying their full milk pails.

Miss Cow was furious! She pulled and she tugged, and she tugged and she pulled. All night long she tried to free herself but it wasn't until daybreak that she finally tugged her horn out of the trunk. And all the time she had been tugging, she had been thinking hard about how to get her own back on that pesky Brer Rabbit. She reckoned he would be coming along that way soon, so she stuck her horn back in the tree trunk. She had got a trick up her sleeve for sure. But that cunning Brer Rabbit returned bright and early and he saw Miss Cow push her horn back in the hole. He smiled to himself. Miss Cow would have to be smarter than that if she was going to catch him out! Then he came strolling by whistling a tune and looking the picture of innocence.

"Morning, Sis Cow," he said, "and how are you this fine morning?"

"Not too good," she said with a groan. "Try as I might, I just can't pull my horn free from this tree."

"Mighty sorry to hear that," said Brer Rabbit. "Perhaps I can help?"

"Perhaps you can," said Miss Cow. "If you stood behind me and pulled my tail real hard, why, you might just pull that horn free."

"Maybe," said Brer Rabbit, "but pulling's thirsty work. I'd need a drink of milk afterwards, if you'd be so kind."

Well, Miss Cow was so mad that Brer Rabbit swore he saw real steam coming from her nostrils! With a loud moo, she pulled her horn from the hole as if from butter. She raced down the meadow after Brer Rabbit and the earth trembled under her hooves. But at the bottom of the field was a large bramble patch and that lucky Rabbit was soon safe inside the bushes. How he laughed. "There isn't one animal I know who can get the better of ole Brer Rabbit!" he boasted happily.

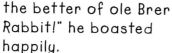

The End